BÊTE NOIRE

FEAR IS JUST A POINT OF VIEW

Editors:

A. W. Gifford
Jennifer L. Gifford

P.O. Box 811
Ortonville, MI 48462

www.betenoiremagazine.com

Bête Noire is published by Dark Opus Press a division of Charm Noir Omnimedia P.O Box 1545, Highland, MI 48357

ISBN: 978-0692324790

In This Issue

Man with a Cigarette

Lawrence Buentello

When Hughes stepped into the room—a downtown walkup more burial crypt than hotel room—a man with a cigarette between his lips was sitting in the old easy chair by the room's lone window. A ribbon of smoke rose above his head, joining the cloud already hovering near the ceiling. The man wore sunglasses and a New York Yankees baseball cap, and, except for appearing to be Caucasian and middle-aged, displayed no memorable features. Hughes had never seen him before, though that wasn't surprising. The man pulled the cigarette from his lips and held it above his lap.

"Close the door," the man said in a soft voice. "We need to talk."

Hughes closed the door.

"I won't ask you to sit," the man continued. "My hope is that we won't be here long enough for it to matter."

Bright daylight shone through the grime on the window glass, obscuring the man's appearance ever further.

"Are you a baseball fan?" Hughes asked, wishing he could sit on the unmade bed in the corner of the room. He'd been walking for an hour, deep in thought, and was tired. But he wasn't tired enough to do what the man with the cigarette wanted him to do.

"A long time ago," the man said. "I'm from here, you know."

"That's understandable. They would need someone familiar with the city."

"You move around a great deal. I decided to wait for you. It seemed logical."

"You should have followed me. You would have seen more of the city."

"I know the city. The city I know is the city I care to know."

"That's the difference between us."

"We're the same, Mr. Hughes. Except for one detail."

Hughes nodded, casting a glance to the bed. He really wished he could sit for a while. He dug his hands into the pockets of his jacket searching for some remnant of the candy he'd bought a few hours ago, a special variety of taffy wrapped in slips of wax paper. He found a single piece in his right pocket, pulled it out and held it up for the man to see.

"Would you like some candy?" he said. "It's excellent, really. My last piece, but I'd like you to have it."

"I don't eat candy, Mr. Hughes."

"Are you sure you wouldn't like to try it?"

"No, thank you. I'm beyond such simple temptations."

Hughes held out the piece of candy a moment longer before shrugging, unwrapping the taffy and slipping it into his mouth.

"You don't know what you're missing," Hughes said around the taffy. "Too bad it's my last piece."

"I'm glad you've been enjoying yourself, but you know it's time to go."

Hughes swallowed the last bit of candy before saying, "Let me ask you something, my friend."

The man shook his head, but Hughes persisted.

"If you're beyond such temptations," Hughes said seriously, "why are you smoking?"

The man glanced briefly at the smoldering cigarette in his fingers, then smiled almost imperceptibly.

"This is my price for doing business," he said. "Why else would I be here? I don't want to be here, after all. But it's nice to smoke again."

The man raised the cigarette to his lips, took a drag and exhaled leisurely.

"Tastes good, doesn't it?" Hughes said. "Is that what did it? The smoking?"

"That's none of your business," the man said. "Are you coming with me?"

"No."

"I'm not leaving this room until you agree."

"I'll find another room."

"You'll find us in every room, Mr. Hughes. You can't hide from us. We'll make things very unpleasant for you."

"You're wasting your time."

"There is order to the universe, Mr. Hughes," the man said. "People like yourself fail to understand that fact. The balance must be maintained. Why is it that you refuse to understand?"

"I understand," Hughes said. "I also disagree with your concept of the order of the universe. The hell with the universe. Maybe if you smoke more cigarettes you'll change your mind."

The man stared at him inscrutably through the dark lenses of his glasses.

"Will you come with me?" he asked again.

"Light another cigarette," Hughes said. "Enjoy yourself. Enjoy the room."

Hughes turned, opened the door and stepped into the hallway. He turned again, then closed the door on the vision of the man with the cigarette. He was tired, but would walk back down to the street. He was infinitely tired, but he would find another place.

Hughes walked for hours after his encounter with the man, disturbed, but undaunted. He didn't return to the room; instead, he found another room two miles away in another nondescript hotel. Money wasn't a problem. He knew how to get money. Privacy was his only problem, now. He wanted to be left alone.

For three days he managed to remain alone, anonymous, and he even began entertaining the thought that they had decided to leave him alone. They couldn't force him to go along with their desires, so perhaps they had given up trying to get him to agree voluntarily. He couldn't fault them, but he hated them for not understanding. How could they not understand?

On the fourth day since his encounter with the smoking man he found himself standing before the window of a store near Times Square, admiring the terribly cheap mementos on display for vacationers searching for tangible trophies of their visit to the city. Junk, all of it, but the shelves of cheap plastic trinkets still brought a smile to his lips. He raised his head and caught his reflection in the window glass. A pale, thirty-five year-old face peered back at him blankly, crowned with reddish eyebrows and adorned with a thin Scandinavian nose. For a moment his corporeality seemed disarming, but then another face appeared in the glass, and he turned, roused from his reverie.

The pretty young woman standing next to him smiled and gestured toward the items glittering behind the window.

"Searching for hidden treasure?" she asked in a pleasant, raspy voice, and Hughes was immediately attracted.

He'd known a woman years before with a similar appearance: curly auburn hair, small, intelligent blue eyes, a sweet smile that never faded despite the vicissitudes of life. That was the other woman, of course. This woman, this stranger, only brought back the memory.

"That depends on your definition of treasure," he said, appraising her from hair to shoes. She was very pretty.

"Anything that catches your fancy, I guess," she said, still smiling. She bent and pressed a small hand against the glass. "This is treasure enough for me. I've always loved window shopping. The act is what's precious to me."

Hughes stared at her reflection in the glass. "You sound like a philosopher."

She raised up and met his gaze. "Simple philosophies are the best. I love window shopping, so I'm out on the street staring into windows. Simple, see?"

"And you're talking to me."

"Yes, I'm talking to you, too. Do you mind?"

He smiled, too. She reminded him of someone else, and he couldn't help but enjoy being in her company.

"I don't mind at all," he said.

"Would you like to get a cup of coffee?" she asked. "I know a place on 45th street."

Her name was Adele, and she worked as an administrative assistant in the Empire State building, high above the tourists and Mahattanites. At first, she hated staring from the windows of an office fifty stories above the ground, but then she got used to the sensation, and grew to love it. She loved the city, its stores and buildings and cantankerous people moving like ocean currents through the endless array of streets. She loved the city's energy, the electricity that brought meaning to an ordinary life.

"Do you live an ordinary life?" Hughes asked her across the small table in the tiny coffee house. His cup of coffee remained untouched; he didn't care for coffee, though he loved good conversation.

She laughed, and even her laugh reminded him of someone else. He enjoyed her laughter, but he may only have been enjoying the memory of someone else's laughter.

"I never considered my life ordinary," she said. "What's ordinary to you may be extraordinary to me. We love what we love."

"I'll certainly agree with that." He glanced around the coffee house, uneasy in the shadows of the place; he felt someone had been watching him, but perhaps that was only his imagination.

"You haven't told me what you do for a living," she said. She sipped her coffee, her second cup, and waited for him to speak before meeting his gaze again.

"I'm retired," he said, disliking the need for exaggeration.

"You're awfully young to be retired. What are you retired from?"

"I've worked a lot of jobs in my life. Good jobs and bad jobs. I guess I'm retired from all of them."

"You make it sound mysterious. Is there some mystery to you I should know about?"

"I'm a pretty ordinary man, I'm afraid. Simple, like you said."

"I don't think you're a simple man. You're a man with secrets."

She smiled, and in her smile he found a portal to another time, another relationship, one he cherished in its time. Hughes had no secrets with *her*; his time with her was the most beautiful experience of his life.

Hughes stared into the woman's eyes, and for the first time he wondered if she was the reason for the suspicion that he was being watched. She was very pretty, anyway.

She reached across the table and touched his hand.

"Would you like to come home with me?" she asked.

He studied her eyes, her familiar blue eyes, and had difficulty separating memory from experience.

"Won't you come with me?"

Hughes sat staring at her for a long time, hating himself for the terrible fear in his heart.

When he left the coffee house, he left alone.

Hughes smelled the smoke even before he opened the door to his room.

The silhouette of a man sat on the edge of the small bed, an ember of burning tobacco bobbing strangely in the dark. Hughes closed the door and found the light switch.

This room was even smaller than his previous room, and held only a single bed and a wooden chair. The window glass was glazed with years of filth and weather. The door to the tiny bathroom stood ajar, the basin's faucet dripping water into a yellowed sink.

The man in the Yankees cap drew another lungful of smoke, then exhaled luxuriously.

Hughes stepped across the room and closed the bathroom door — he hated the sound of dripping water.

"I told you that you couldn't hide from us," the man said, crossing his legs. He still wore sunglasses, despite the time of night. Hughes thought of old film noire movies, seen on a black and white television.

"It took you long enough to find me again," he said. "I find that curious."

Hughes moved into the room, wondering where else he could sleep for the night. He had no intention of sharing the room.

"Aren't you weary of this charade?" said the man with the cigarette.

Hughes stood staring down at the man. "Was she one of you?"

The man inhaled through his cigarette again, exhaled slowly.

"Who?"

"The woman I met today. Was she one of you?"

"It's nice that you met someone. I wonder who you met?"

"She was one of you."

"How do you know?"

"What she said. She said —"

Hughes turned away and stared at the grimy window glass. How could he be certain? What if —

"You're playing with my memory," Hughes said without turning. "Enticing me in different ways. Is that how it's going to be?"

"What memories, Mr. Hughes?"

"Memories that mean something to me. Enticements."

"I know *exactly* what you mean," the man said. "What's more important to you? Experience, or memory?"

"What's the difference?"

"Experience happens on a moment to moment basis. But a memory can be reviewed any time. What's more important to you, experiences that haven't yet happened to you, or recalling the memory of experiences that actually *mean* something to you?"

"You're trying to confuse me."

"Consider it."

Hughes thought about Adele, and he thought of the woman she reminded him of, and wondered which perception meant more to him. Something that goes on, or something that already happened —

"Why won't you leave me alone," he said. He reached into his pocket for a piece of candy, but found none. The lack of candy bothered him immensely, though he didn't know why it should.

"You know why we can't let you stay," the man replied.

"Leave me alone."

"You *are* alone, Mr. Hughes. If you come with me, you won't be alone any longer. Won't you come with me tonight?"

"No."

"You'll always have your memories. Those memories you love."

"No, it isn't the same. It *isn't*."

Hughes turned away from the window and stepped to the door. For a moment his hand lingered on the doorknob, and he wondered if he always *would* have his memories. But wouldn't they steal those, too? If they were going to take the *experiences*, wouldn't they take the *memories*, too?

Hughes opened the door.

"I *do* like smoking cigarettes," he heard the man say as he stepped into the hallway.

"I won't go with you," he said as he began walking toward the stairs.

"We'll see you in your dreams, Mr. Hughes."

They did, too.

Lawrence Buentello has published over 80 short stories in a variety of genres, and is a Pushcart Prize nominee. He lives in San Antonio, Texas.

The Death in Me

Wesley D. Gray

My wife smells the death in me
while her belly swells
with death's contradiction.
She sniffs at cheek and lip;
the vapor lingers on fingers,
sticks to me like dew on petals,
and leaks from pores like nectar.

It comes to me now as a wound
in the moist flesh of my mouth,
an ulcer burning like a sun,
a screaming scorpion to remind me
of all I have to lose.

Infection creeps from my throat,
rotting hands reaching out,
as fingers curl around my face,
prying my jaw wide.

The thing I've bred emerges,
bringing pain
as it flays me open.

Then it stands before me,
more than just disease,
for now I see
I have birthed a creature--
Living Death returns to reap me,
to cleanse me,
and take me home.

Wesley D. Gray is a writer, an author of fiction, and a self-proclaimed poet. His chapbook, Come Fly with Death: Poems Inspired by the Artwork of Zdzislaw Beksinski *is available now. If you're ready to delve deeper, be sure to visit his blog,* Marrowroot.com.

Raven

Anna Sykora

she left her skin
in the rumpled bed
along with a single
raven feather

proof of their
married years together
and the man howled
loud and long

and the children wailed
like wind in november
bit their hands
and bloodied the doorway

no I will never
return not ever
this mother you
never have known

Anna Sykora *has been an attorney in NYC and teacher of English in Germany, where she resides with her patient husband and three enormous cats. To date she has placed 345 poems and 131 tales, mostly genre, in the small press... Motto: eat your rejections like pretzels; writing is the joy.*

Das Requiem

Matt Andrew

The ashes of the last women's orchestra were still floating down from the smoldering chimneys when Zofia stepped onto the wooden platform. She wiped the wet cinders—infused with drifting snow-flakes—from her shoulders, but only spread the gritty carbon on her fingertips while more fell to replace them. Zofia braced her tired frame against the podium while the new group of women, all in matching striped tunics, inspected the instruments they had inherited.

The ladies settled into their seats, broken crates sunken into the muddy turf. The cold wind blew through the square, nipping at Zofia's cracked lips and hands. Her fingers stung, sticking to the icy steel cap of the baton.

A line of prisoners passed through the square and disappeared into the gloomy arched passageway of a large brick building. Guards barked guttural commands at the dazed civilians while they trudged through the mud like cattle.

The two enormous steel chimneys, so tall they seemed to scrape the gray clouds, sprouted from the back of the brick structure. The ashes that floated onto Zofia's shoulders were redolent of the burnt wood or hot coal of Poland's mining towns, but she wondered if she knew the people they used to be. Had they ever talked to one another, or shared a bread ration? She knocked more of the soot off, smearing the slag into her palms and spreading charcoal slashes down her arms.

Some of the prisoners carried luggage, only to have it tossed out of a side door after the owner vanished into the tunnel. Two Jews sorted through the belongings. One gray-haired lady left her place in the orchestra and rummaged through the pile of discarded baggage, returning to the group with an antique violin.

The commandant stood watching the women, tucked in his black overcoat with a riding crop under his arm. His stiff, Aryan poise and wraith-like countenance suggested Death himself.

He used the orchestras to sooth the parade of slumped, confused prisoners while they were herded into oblivion. He detested the dissonance of guards and captives, alike — the moans, pleads, curses, and the punchy staccato of pistol shots. The commandant was the maestro of their last operas, preferring a quiet adagio with a satisfying finale of Zyklon-B.

The women tuned their violins and cellos with trembling fingers. The old woman cradling the tarnished flute muttered to herself and nibbled a bread crust. With their jutting collarbones, bony arms, and sunken eyes, they were an orchestra of living dead.

A hand grasped Zofia's arm and pulled her from the platform. A tall SS officer, in his jet-black uniform and phallic helmet, stood over her.

"The commandant wants *Madame Butterfly*. All three movements. You know it, yes?"

He pushed a folder, crammed with loose papers, into her hands.

"*Madame Butterfly*, Sturmbannführer?" Zofia looked past the officer. The woman she shared a straw mattress with, whose name she avoided, shuffled past in the line of prisoners, prodded by a rifle butt. "Yes, I think."

"Do you!?" he screamed, shaking her by her frail arm so hard her loose teeth clacked together and she bit her tongue, tasting warm copper. He pulled a pistol from his holster and pointed it in her face.

"Yes! Yes, Sturmbannführer!"

He pushed her back toward the platform. Zofia hobbled around the musicians on their crates and passed the sheets out to the ensemble. They laid them in their laps or against the backs of the woman in front of them and leafed through the papers, squinting, shaking their heads, or looking at Zofia with hands held up. The text on the browned sheet music was printed in English, German, Italian, and one even in Japanese. Notes and symbols had faded into grey, moldy blemishes having sat in wet basements or desk drawers, unused for decades.

The commandant cleared his throat and twirled his finger. Zofia stepped back up onto the podium. She tapped it with the baton and began.

They staggered through the first few measures, none in sync, twenty women all playing a screeching, bastardized version of what they saw on the papers. They ignored Zofia's efforts to keep them in time. She shook her head and waved her hands while trying to direct.

Violins screeched across dry strings. The flutes were off-beat, flat whistles. An old woman that Zofia was sure was partly deaf, her cello braced between knobby knees, only hung her head and sobbed.

The commandant huffed angry clouds of frost from his nostrils and whispered to the other officers that stood with him. He pointed at the line of prisoners beside them. The officer walked toward Zofia, smirking, jackboots slinging mud with each step.

"No! Try another," whispered a young woman with a black eye in front of Zofia. She held a viola up to her chin, cushioned with a lavender swatch of cloth against the chinrest. "Do Bach's second Brandenberg. Everyone knows that one."

Zofia leaned against the podium and the baton dropped to her side. The only decision she wanted to make was how to get to her beloved Hiram, already in peaceful *shamayim,* the quickest.

Step into the line that would deliver her into the bowels of the chimneys?

Stab the officer through the eye with the baton and be shot immediately (God willing)?

The officer shouted to a group of guards and pointed at the musicians.

"Please! For all our sakes," whispered the young woman. Her eyes were wide and darted between Zofia and the approaching tide of black.

Zofia used her last few seconds, or the fifteen or so paces between the officer and the platform, to think of Hiram and their children. Hiram and his graying, full beard with hand carved pipe. Radda and Anna practicing the Goldberg Variations on their Wurlitzer.

The officer, long strides closing the distance, pulled his pistol. Zofia could hear the metallic *rack* when he chambered the first round.

A burst of sweet, bouncing notes startled Zofia from her memories.

The young woman with the viola was playing the opening measures of Bach with passion, as if an audition, and looked to her fellow musicians to join in. The strings joined, one at a time, all in unison, followed by flutes and clarinet. Even the hard of hearing cello player picked up on the floating melody of the Second Brandenburg.

The viola player looked up at Zofia, eyes still wide, urgent, silently demanding that Zofia lead them.

"Wait," yelled the commandant.

The officer stopped and looked back. The commandant waved him over. All the guards in the square, formerly cursing and abusing the condemned prisoners, had turned their attention to the music of their Teutonic kinsman.

Zofia raised her baton and took control of the orchestra. She watched the young viola player. The girl's eyes were closed and she stroked the chords elegantly, her lavender cloth graying in the ashen rain.

Zofia wasn't sure if the daily terror she would endure was worth the gift of quiet that the prisoners would have during the last hundred feet they would ever walk, but she knew Hiram would nod his head and gesture with his pipe, urging her to play on.

For all their sakes, she would.

Matt Andrew *is a former U.S. Marine who works in the banking sector in Dallas. His fiction can also be read in* Pantheon Magazine, Plan B Magazine, *and the upcoming* State of Horror: North Carolina *anthology.*

At The Midpoint Between Heaven And Hell in a Dismal Barroom

J. J. Steinfeld

Heavenly has nothing to do with Heaven
because there is no damn Heaven,
you whisper before your first drink
philosophy and theology and predictions
of vile discoveries and vulgar endings
will come later, second or third drink,
the night is young, your intellect
hardly lubricated, apocalyptic chatter awaits.
On some nights revelations and wisdom
flow early before your drinking partner
talks of self-destruction or rebirth
or a deep understanding of nothing
and its multiplicity of corollaries
even of compassion and love and regret
like cheap food additives gone poisonous
the conversational mix more than madness
the darkness cultivated, refined, redefined,
and magically misshaped, further darkened.
I know I'm not qualified to deal with your mind

but what the heck, have another drink on me
you've earned it, what with your stirring avoidance
and marvellous sidestepping all so eloquently displayed.
As I leave, eager for silence and escape,
I hear you order another drink
and yell into the dismal barroom,
Hellish has nothing to do with Hell
because there is no damn Hell...

Canadian poet, fiction writer, and playwright J. J. Steinfeld *lives on Prince Edward Island, where he is patiently waiting for Godot's arrival and a phone call from Kafka. While waiting, he has published fourteen books, including* Should the Word Hell Be Capitalized? *(Stories, Gaspereau Press),* Would You Hide Me? *(Stories, Gaspereau Press),* An Affection for Precipices *(Poetry, Serengeti Press),* Misshapenness *(Poetry, Ekstasis Editions),* Word Burials *(Novel and Stories, Crossing Chaos Enigmatic Ink), and* A Glass Shard and Memory *(Stories, Recliner Books). More than three hundred of his short stories and nearly six hundred poems have appeared in anthologies and periodicals internationally, and over forty of his one-act plays and a handful of full-length plays have been performed in Canada and the United States.*

WILL OF THE SHAPESHIFTER

James Frederick William Rowe

The flesh will yield if the spirit is focused
As the mind is malleable so too shall the meat be made
For the body is but the vessel of the spirit
And my spirit is mighty with my will triumphant!

So proceeds the metamorphosis of my alchemy of flesh:
Bones creak like groaning timber as they knit to new shapes
A pitiful protest before they submit to their remolding
The pain does not even arouse my regard

The skin stains and darkens without kiss of the sun
In places hair sprouts, in others is shed
And a spat shower of displaced teeth heralds
A dental usurpation by a set sharp and shining

Blossoming capillaries surge with fresh blood
While muscles bulge to new contours, depress to new curves
Finally, a face smeared into a new clarity
Emerges to greet a mirror held with delight

Flawless - such is the handiwork of my will
A transmigration by transubstantiation
I am master over form, victor over matter
Mother and father to a new birth: my own

What place do I hold in the natural order?
Fool! I have snapped the chain of being!
Confined to a single suit of skin, you are but an animal
I am Panmorphos, of all forms, and I am God over flesh!

James Frederick William Rowe *is a Rhysling-nominated poet and author out of Brooklyn, New York. In the last few years, he has cut out a substantial niche in the speculative poetry front, having seen over twenty-five poems published internationally in such markets as* Big Pulp, Songs of Eretz, Tale of the Talisman, Heroic Fantasy Quarterly, Andromeda Spaceways In-flight Magazine, *and now* Bete Noire. *When he is not writing verses and crafting yarns, he is employed as an adjunct professor of philosophy in the City University of New York, is pursuing a Ph.D. in the same subject, and works a variety of freelance positions.*

The poet's website can be found at http://jamesfwrowe.wordpress.com

ROOT TRANSFORMATION   *by Denny E. Marshall*

Denny E Marshall *has had art, poetry and fiction published, some recently.*
He is just an average person. He does not know anyone famous.

PUPPET CORPS

Joshua L. Hood

The final battalion marched across the front line for the first time in a dozen years. The sky above the city had been red for a long, long time. Soldiers had begun taking pills to keep the stench of decomposition from disturbing the proceedings around them. Now the ground was more canvas and flesh than it was dirt. The rucksacks were the biggest problem. Both sides had stopped wearing them long ago, but so many fully outfitted bodies still lay on the ground in the kill-zone that it looked like a boulder field in the red sunsets. That made it hard for the puppets to walk, they'd been tripping over debris more and more as the years went by. No one picked up the bodies anymore. The field-sweepers had long ago been drafted into the battalion, just as had the engineers, the doctors, the scientists who'd invented the pills, and even the commanders. For the past decade or so the war was no longer the clean, organized affair that it had evolved into during its middle years.

Vox watched as one of his puppets neared the mangled corpse of one of its fallen comrades. The corpse wasn't destroyed enough to avoid the effects of the array. It was kicking its broken legs into the air as it tried to walk, the arch of its spine propped its head up off the ground as though it stooped to avoid gunfire.

Vox saw what was coming and straightened himself as quickly as possible. All across the hundred miles of front line, a hundred thousand puppets shot bolt upright and stopped moving along with him. Random and distant shots sounded as several hundred of them toppled at the sudden cessation of movement. The puppet who he'd tried to stop from tripping had already caught its foot on the rim of the corpse's helmet, and despite the leader's attempt to prevent it, the puppet fell to the ground, sending a dozen rounds from its rifle into the back of the soldier ahead of it. Vox cursed, rookie move. Better to let one puppet flounder than to topple a thousand more. Who knows how many had been shot by that bungle. Some may have even died, though he doubted it. The puppets only fired a dozen shots when they fell, a poorly implemented defensive protocol, and it would take more than that to stop one of their own kind.

Predictably, the fallen soldier stood back up while its comrade who it'd shot several times simply stood there as though nothing had happened. Vox shook his head and a hundred thousand dead soldiers pantomimed along. He hoped that the enemy Vox was having better luck.

It all started with those damned pills.

Because of the stench, they invented the pills, and because of the pills they invented the field-sweepers. The sweepers needed a smooth place to harvest their corpses, so they flattened the kill-zone. Once the puppet-arrays had been installed it was easier to just keep the front-line where it was and use the flattened field to march small patrols up to the city. Puppets were clumsy and imprecise. To actually have entered the city, or to have moved the frontline, would have meant flattening more ground, and there simply wasn't time for that.

Vox was there when Smitty had first given the brass the idea for puppets. He wasn't Vox then, that would come later. Way back then he was just a Corporal Abernath. Smitty was the original Vox, given that honor because he was the first one to think of lashing together a few corpses as a meat-shield for his patrol's advance. They'd used shoelaces and para-cord. That was back when they were fully outfitted and actually had para-cord. Vox looked down. Velcro. *When did they stop issuing shoelaces?*

He suddenly realized that if the enemy Vox was watching him right then that he or she would realize that he wasn't paying attention, so he looked up from his shoes and fired a few shots in three different directions. The puppets looked up and did the same. *That'll throw 'em off.*

Smitty's dead soldier phalanx had worked perfectly. Aberanth, Smitty and half a dozen other soldiers whose names' were lost, had heaved the wall of rot-less corpses forward across the battlefield and into the city. The patrol had gained half a mile that way. That was back when they would still cross the front line. Leadership was so impressed that they asked the scientists to invent a way, a microchip or something, which would make the corpses stand along the front line and take shots rather than just lay there all useless like. The scientists consented and they came up with the puppet-array. Back then it was only a solid beam of transmission. All the troops had the chip implanted along with a little battery that would power their bodies for up to one mile when they died. Once they reached the beam, they would stop and pile up like a fortification. If the frontline moved, then they just moved the beam and all the dead soldiers would hop up and reinforce the new battle lines.

That worked so well that they began putting in bigger batteries and giving the corpses explosives. After that everyone whose draft number started with A through G became a sapper. That's how Smitty ended up when the first puppets shot him dead.

Vox hesitated at the edge of the city. Already half his force was piled up against the outside walls of the buildings, unable to circumvent them. The canvas scuffling of thousands of cold bodies rustled with every step he took as they helplessly tried to march along with him. He looked deep into the shadows. He'd forgotten what a proper building looked like and the city did no good in reminding him. There wasn't a right angle within a hundred miles of that place. The enemy puppets were lying on the ground, all in the same position and mostly motionless, but occasionally twitching. He took that as a good sign. If the enemy Vox did still survive, then he or she wasn't on the defensive, maybe sleeping. Of course, any further into the city and it would only take the enemy Vox's standing up to realize that he was surrounded. There really was no good way to tell the difference between a dead corpse and a sleeping puppet.

Within the year they had broadened the beam of the puppet-array into a cone shaped transmission pointed directly at the city. The original scientists had all either been drafted or succumb to radiation poisoning, but the new wave seemed just as competent. They'd heard that Smitty was responsible for the innovation of puppet warfare and, in perhaps the last sentimental gesture in the whole of humanity, they recruited him to be the first Vox Mortua.

Corporal Abernath was present at the first trial. He could still remember the way that Smitty smiled proudly as the bent and decrepit scientist attached the probes and diodes to his scalp with their warty, radioactive hands. The corporal had a bad feeling about it even then, but it was hard not to have bad feelings about reanimating half a dozen dead soldiers to follow every move you made. Even now, long after Corporal Abernath became the last Vox, it still gave him the shivers.

The cone shaped beam clicked on invisibly and six dead soldiers rose to their feet almost as if they were alive. They weren't, never would be again – you can't beat death – but they would do well enough for the trick. Smitty and the scientists were ecstatic.

The experiment was happening far behind the lines, but the enemy was shrewd. A private in their own battalion, a spy, was broadcasting a feed of the whole experiment. Corporal Abernath was the first to notice. He was the only one not celebrating the unrivalled success of the creatures that would from thence forth be known as puppets. Abernath didn't have a rifle. He was off duty, and rifles never left the battlefield. Smitty and the puppets, on the other hand, were fully outfitted for the experiment.

He was quick on the trigger, Smitty, splattering the spy all over the tent flap before she could finalize the transmission. At the same time all of the puppets raised their rifles and fired directly ahead of them. Three scientists and Smitty were casualties of their own success. Smitty, followed by the six corpses, got up and went running toward the front line, disappearing into the smoke of a new offensive and exploding distantly as just one more pop among many. That's when they realized the significance of the fact that, even at the frontlines, not everyone dies facing the same direction.

⸰✠⸰

Vox turned and looked at the legion of corpses behind him. They still faced forward. That was the one action that he could take that they couldn't pantomime. No matter what he did, they would always face the frontline.

He took a single step forward. The unbroken silence was shattered by the sound of a hundred thousand feet tapping to the ground all around him. The puppets jammed up on the buildings struggled futilely to move into the city. Those who weren't confronted by obstacles advanced with him. He knelt down to look the body of an enemy soldier. The receiver from enemy's own puppet array jutted out from its skull where a bullet had removed the outer half of its head. The rest of the face was impassive, blank though slightly snarling in a way that

meant that this soldier had been dead for a long time. The enemy
hadn't been cleaning up their dead either.

❦

Vox had been watching for months. He'd concluded that there was
only one enemy left alive, a Vox, his own counterpart. There was no
variation amongst the soldiers in the city, how they moved, how they
stumbled and fell. He'd seen them hedging forward for several weeks,
but always waiting to go on the defense, never attacking. Vox had
been doing the same. Though there were legions of moving bodies
along this stretch of the frontline, there were only two sets of movements ever to be seen.

One day Vox got bored and waved at the enemy. He didn't know
why, maybe he was lonely. He knew that if the enemy waved back
that the Vox was waiting out there too, watching. At first nothing
happened. Vox slumped in disappointment and sat down in a chair. It
was something he rarely did, since it would be very unlikely that any
of the puppets would be fortunately positioned in front of a chair, but
he was bored and tired. All at once a hundred thousand corpses tried
to sit down and flopped clumsily to the ground. Bullets whizzed into
the city.

A movement was perceptible from behind some of the buildings. He
flicked on image enhancement and saw that all the corpses in the
shadows appeared to be laughing. He couldn't help but smile. He
wasn't alone after all.

❦

Eventually he stopped seeing the enemy forces altogether. He knew
it could have been a trick to lure him to into the city, but he didn't
care. He knew there was at least one other living thing in the world,
and wanted to know what happened to it.

❦

Colonel Vox Mortua Abernath had gained prestige as his single
patrol of puppets grew into a legion. It didn't take long for the enemy
to gain puppet technology, but it was rough. The city didn't accom-
modate the strategy well. They were falling by the hundreds to the
lethal force of the array, even if the puppets relied on accuracy by luck
and volume. The enemy had developed a strategy to combat the puppets, though. They quickly learned the first rule of puppetry – as does

the corpse, so does the soldier. If the puppets were reloading, then Vox was out of ammo. If the puppets were sneezing, then Vox was distracted. If the puppets were squatting on the field with their pants down, then Vox was taking a shit. It was a matter of easy strategic evolution to watch for details. Corpses were clumsy when they reloaded, they didn't sneeze and they didn't shit. Just aim at the one emitting effluence and pull the trigger – a dozen guns silenced. Vox's learned very quickly not to even glance behind them lest the gesture give them away.

Brass had an easy solution for that one too. Just have the link jump to the next nearest Vox. Soon enough the best puppet-masters had huge forces amassed behind them. Abernath was the best, and luckiest, of all. He'd gained considerable reputation before the tide of war washed away the soldiers like grains of sand. Soon enough, all of those who'd lauded and praised him fell into line behind him until he was the only living body in the world.

Except, just perhaps, for the enemy Vox, lying in wait somewhere beyond that crumble of buildings.

He sighed heavily and a puppet close behind him pantomimed a huffed breath that was the closest that the corpses ever got to speaking. Speech was the one thing that the scientists couldn't get the dead soldiers to emulate – hence why the leader of each troop was called Vox Mortua. Voice of the Dead.

He'd gone at least a mile into the city and the litter of enemy corpses had grown sparse. The buildings there were better intact, but the air raids of decades ago had left them smashed up all the same. At the end of the street was a building with large banners hanging from it. There were clean spots on the unbroken windows as though someone had used their hand to clear away the dust to get a better look out. The insignia on the banners was that of the enemy high command. If the last enemy Vox was anywhere, it'd be here.

He started walking toward it. Several faint echoes of gunfire went off behind him as more of his puppets tripped and fell in the distance. He wondered how far the puppet-arrays reached into the city. At any moment he could come to the end of their signal and the connection would be severed. That was instant death for a Vox.

In the early days too many soldiers had their wills frayed by being constantly mocked in every movement by growing numbers of their dead allies. Some had tried to unplug, and so the scientists put a Fail-Safe-Kill-Switch into the connections. Getting your FSKS circuit installed became known as "getting your first kiss." The unspoken end of that sentence was "of death." Once you became a Vox, you would always be one – until the whole world followed behind you.

Vox walked up the stairs to the command building. There was blood on the stairs, a trail leading up to the door. It wasn't wet, but still sticky. The door handle was covered in the same blood as the steps. The door was ajar.

He noticed that the puppets around him became sluggish and less responsive, the connection was weakening. Only three puppets made it up the stairs without falling. He suddenly felt a strange fondness for the dead people following him. In the sparse company of those who'd been hearty enough to make it through the city with him he felt like he was part of an actual companionship again, a band of brothers. He looked into the dead, leathery faces of his soldiers. He had to turn around completely so that they wouldn't copy his movements. He knew that made him a perfect target for anyone watching from inside the building, but somehow he knew that no one was. He almost sighed again, but didn't like the way that the corpses tried to emulate his breathing so instead he just went into the building.

The blood trail led directly to the middle of a large marble room. The whole ground floor was bare except for some furniture at a guard post, long abandon. The floor was ornate with the art of a civilization far gone. The colors that weren't red caught Vox's attention in a familiar sort of way, but he looked away before he could remember where he'd seen them last.

In the middle of the room, surrounded by the blood, was the form of a person who'd been covered in a green blanket. She wasn't dead, the blanket rose and fell unevenly. Unless she was a puppet and the Vox was upstairs sleeping, but that was unlikely, puppets didn't bleed.

A single corpse stood behind him. The other two that had made it up the stairs had jammed up on the door frame when he entered. Of the hundred thousand left, only one had made the journey with its commander. The feeling of comradery came back over him, but then there was suddenly repulsion too. This thing was not his brother. It wasn't even looking him in the eye. He raised his gun and watched the puppet do the same. He lowered it, and so did the puppet. The dead eyes of the corpse were still staring at the breathing form of the injured woman on the floor. It couldn't turn its head backward like Vox had, and that was the only thing that separated the two.

Vox shot it in the chest. The corpse soldier fired a round impotently into the marble wall forty-five degrees to its left, as far as it could go. A hundred thousand shots echoed from outside. Vox shot it again, this time in the leg. The bone shattered and the puppet slumped sideways, but the atrophied muscle and tissue kept it on its feet.

The woman on the floor made a sound. It wasn't intelligible, but it was alive. Vox emptied the rest of his clip into the skull of his most loyal puppet and it finally fell to the ground, disconnected from the array. He toed it until it rolled over and read the name tag on its chest. No one he knew. Good.

The woman made another noise. Vox saw her move a hand out from under the green blanket. There was a pistol in the hand. She took a wild shot in his direction. A hundred thousand shots echoed from outside the building. Vox smiled at the effort. He rounded to the unarmed side of the woman and looked down. She was wounded, bad. Three ribs were sticking up and making little bumps in the blanket. The side of her face was raw and ripped away like someone had taken sandpaper to it.

The faint sound of a hundred thousand guns being reloaded filtered through the marble walls as Vox snapped another magazine into his rifle. *So this is victory.*

The woman looked up at him with the exact opposite thought. *So this is defeat.* After a long time Vox lowered his rifle. The woman didn't look relieved. He knew that a few more paces toward the far wall would disconnect him from the array and he would die. If she'd only managed to crawl a little further back, maybe behind that old metal security desk, she would have won. That wasn't fair.

He dropped his rifle onto the marble floor. The clack of two rifles hitting the stoop came through the open door and echoed around the room, washing out the sound of all the others in the distance. The shoulder of one of the two puppets was visible behind the door frame. Vox sneered at it. The woman looked toward the door too. Vox took off his helmet and pulled his head back, then whipped it forward. They heard the squelching sound of lifeless heads slamming into the rattling door frame. He did it again, and again, until the puppets collapsed from neurological trauma. He smiled at the woman. She softened a little, but then winced in pain. He knelt at her side.

The sound of a hundred thousand guns clattering to the ground nearby filtered through the marble as she released hold on her pistol.

"What happened?" Vox asked.

"I fell," she replied.

"Ouch," Vox said.

"Yeah," she replied.

"I've put a bomb on our array," Vox told her for some reason.

"Okay."

"I don't want to be followed by armies of the dead anymore."

"Me neither."

"When it blows, I'll disconnect. I'll be dead soon."

"Welcome to the club."

Vox smiled. "Care for some company?"

"Sure."

She groaned with pain as Vox lifted the edge of the blanket and slid in beside her. The marble was cold and hard, but it felt good to find a warm body.

Joshua L. Hood *lives in Boise, Idaho. He's been writing and illustrating for several years and is thrilled to be included in this issue of Bete Noire, a publication of which he's been a long time fan. Aside from this, he can most recently be found in the anthology* Cadavers *from KnightWatch Press. He's also appeared (writing and illustration) in* Encounters Magazine, Horrorbound.com, Chilling Tales for Dark Nights *and various other spooky story outlets. For a full dose of Josh's writing look for his anthology* Melting People *available through major book sellers, or go to* www.joshualhood.com *for more.*

MELTING PEOPLE

Ghosts, demons,
madness,
a late night gas station
where people melt
like wax...

This eclectic anthology
has classic horror,
science fiction, drama
and everything in
between.

Worlds of mystery
lies within these
pages, waiting for you
to come in and explore
the strangeness!

11 short stories of the bizarre and unexpected by

JOSHUA L. HOOD

The Aviaries of God

Doug D'Elia

The presence of creatures
with wings is terrifying.
It shouldn't be
but it is.

Murder's of them, noisy
high shrilled cackling
in strange unknown dialects,

dark feathery raven wings
attached to perfect bodies
with grotesque strangeness,

and black Iroquois hair
slicked back, like a hood,
floating in dark corners
longing to come to Earth
to entertain unaware.

As if they could help anyway.

Doug D'Elia *was born in Massachusetts. He graduated from the University of Central Florida with a major in Philosophy and Religion.*
He saw his first angels in the hospitals serving Vietnam casualties. He is the author of 4 books. A list of all his published work and projects an be found at dougdelia.com

LOVE: APOCALYPTIC

Chad Stroup

Everything was melting and glistening. The sun hadn't set for a couple of months. Sometimes I swore I could see the ground pulsing like it had developed a healthy set of lungs. I was afraid standing still too long on the asphalt would make the sole of my shoe stick to it and create the world's worst tasting S'more. I wouldn't have picked up a quarter I found on the street if you dared me.

⋘✠⋙

"Adam, do you ever wonder what it might feel like to just slide right off?"

It had been less than a week since I met Dell, but I could already tell that she didn't care for me very much. Why else would she have been scooting to the edge of the roof, contemplating the pros and cons of ending it all?

"Could be any easy out," I said. "Hello, Heaven—let me in! Is that what you're thinking? Nice try. Too many variables, though."

Dell edged her rump closer to a possible doom. "It's about a fifty foot drop, right? From this high up, it's pretty much a done deal."

"No way. There's so much to consider. The slope, what part of your body you'd land on, the fact that it's pure concrete down there instead of pillows and teddy bears."

"Sounds like it's as good a shot as any."

I knew she was taunting me, testing me. Seeing if I would have been able to handle the inevitable loneliness. She knew she had all the time in the world to screw with my head. Sure was good at it, too. She did it professionally. Before.

"Not really. Too high of a chance you might survive the fall and end up badly injured or paralyzed. That'd have to be worse than your current situation, right?"

Dell shrugged.

We barely attempted to carry on any meaningful conversations after leeching onto each other. I guess that was mostly my fault. Never was much good at anything beyond small talk and failed one-liners. The desperation should have inspired some sort of change in my approach. Nope. I first spotted her scavenging in the same GoodFoods I had been scoping out all day. I was hoping to score some stale JuJubes or something equally nutritious. Our eyes met in the baking aisle of all places. Then, just as quickly, she averted her eyes. It was like a fragrance advertisement gone horribly wrong.

She should have been pleased to see me. To see *anyone*. There wasn't a lot of socializing going on. No tech. No virtual. Just real, raw life shitting its anal FroYo all over us.

"Do you...*did* you have any kids, Dell?"

"No. Stephen never wanted them."

"Stephen?"

"My husband."

Dell's face was an impenetrable fortress, but I could tell there was a flood on the other side doing its best to break down the gates.

"Oh. That's too bad. You'd pump out some decent looking little pups." I nudged her shoulder with my elbow. I never did well with sensitive moments and I was even more terrible at flirting. Blame the Internet. I had a big set of Cyber Nuts. The worst relationship dilemma I ever experienced before was a friend request denial, but I just moved on to the next set of pixelated images, trying to determine if the latest babe I was stalking was actually a SIF or not. Strategic camera angles were no longer an option. Did the World Wide Web still exist even though there was nothing to power it up? And why did this bother me either way? Shouldn't I have still been moving on?

But Dell, she was a lot more sophisticated than any of the immature chicks I dealt with in the "olden days," which I admit was very intimidating.

"You ever miss making out like middle-schoolers?" I asked her. I couldn't have been any less subtle. She just gracefully ignored me. *Not if he's the last guy on Earth*, she probably thought.

Except there was just one problem—that's exactly what I was.

Well, that may not have been entirely accurate. Hard to say. I didn't exactly have any direct contact with anyone in Malaysia, Poland, Uruguay, Libya, or—hell, even Bakersfield. But I felt pretty confident that I was the last fuckable guy in Los Angeles County. The only other sentient life I had seen in weeks were the Sloogs, and trust me—no sane woman would have wanted a soggy Sloog pecker anywhere near their lady flower. I accidentally saw one of those way too up close and personal once; it was like a rotten pickle dipped in peach marmalade.

Speaking of peach, it's not like Dell was some blue-ribbon cobbler either. I mean, don't get me wrong—she would have done in a pinch. And this was sure as hell the tightest pinch that Little Adam had ever been in. I wouldn't have even needed beer goggles. Hell, I wish that option had even existed at that point. Booze was the first thing to get looted in the early days. But Dell, she had a certain charm about her. Or maybe I was just getting desperately horny.

Did I mention she was almost twenty years older than me? I didn't have a problem with that. Hidden pink parts don't have crow's feet.

"Look, maybe it's too soon," I said, "but maybe we should, you know, try to keep each other warm later. If you catch my drift."

"You know, I'd almost consider taking you up on that offer if your body had a built in air conditioner instead."

"I know you might have some issues with my youth. Time to get over it, Dell. May/December romances won't be frowned upon in a doomed world. It all comes down to options, options, options."

"Hmm...virtuous virility, I presume?"

"I don't follow you."

Dell's gaze kept drifting back to the sky. The clouds were purple, thin, and feathery, like some randy angels had a pillow fight and then spilled a 2-Liter bottle of grape soda.

"It's kind of nice out," I said to Dell. Or to myself. "The sun's almost hidden today. Or tonight. Do you have any idea when it is?"

"No. I lost track of time a few days after the stars went missing."

"Alexander Graham Bell would not be pleased."

Dell groaned. "I think you've got your inventors mix—"

Suddenly there was a loud and obnoxious bubbling sound below us, like a flash mob whose schtick involved gargling tapioca pudding.

Dell looked down and her expression darkened. It was one of those brief moments where her wrinkles showed.

"We'd better get inside," she said. Her voice dropped to a whisper. "Those Sloogs are way too close for comfort. They're forming one of those organized groups down there again."

I thought it was kind of cute that she at least took on the nickname I gave to those muties. Really though, it's not like she could have come up with something better to call a group of freaks that had once been human, but ended up looking like giant, slithering slices of moldy pizza.

"Okay. I'll meet you in there in a sec."

Dell waddled her middle-aged bod toward the stairs and I sneaked a peek at the rear view. She definitely did her fair share of Pilates in her day. I peered over the edge of the roof and caught the Sloogs climbing and sliming all over each other, forming a bastardized totem pole. It looked like a mucous candle liquefying in the sun.

Before I went inside, I grabbed a small stone that had been cooling in a precious patch of shade and tossed it as far as I could away from the Sloogs. After a few seconds I heard it crash into something. A trash-can, the hood of a car, a gate, didn't really matter. The important thing is that it completely rerouted those breathing bruised bananas. Sent them away from our hideout. Temporarily. They scattered off like conspiring roaches startled by sudden light in the kitchen.

The sound echoed and jarred me. Obviously, this used to be a pretty busy city. Everything was abandoned. Desolate. Lonely.

Boo fucking hoo.

Most days it was so silent you could hear a mouse dropping a deuce. So the crash of the stone sounded epic, like the world ending. God, what a terrible analogy. Too soon?

I finally followed Dell back into the apartment complex we had been shacking up in. Anything indoors was pretty wonderful since we didn't have a lot of options for shade. If I was in the sun too long I started feeling like a piece of bacon, and I was not quite ready to start gnawing on myself. During the waking hours we hung out in the rec room on the third floor since there were a couple of nice comfy couches and a pool table. Quite a luxury, for sure, but I wish there had been foosball or air hockey instead. I guess the felt on the pool table made it a comparatively quieter pastime, though. We sure didn't want to attract any unwanted company. We were making wagers back and forth with the same tattered bills and weathered coins. Kinda funny how brazen I was with money in a world where it didn't matter any-more. A far cry from my days as a bike courier, when currency was cherished and I was willing to make some deliveries that weren't ex-actly on the up and up. Gee, I could have been anyone after the apoca-lypse! Reinvented myself! How special.

We had a decent stockpile of bottled water, so we usually split one during a game. Best. Invention. Ever. Thanks, 18th Century Europe.

There was a chalkboard next to the pool table. A few names were scrawled on it—presumably those who were next in line for a proper game of billiards right before everything fell apart. I had to wonder what happened to "Romeo Shadduck." With a name like that, he had to have been a hustler. Probably just became a Dustler like the rest of the world. Or "Maynard K." Just the last initial. Did this imply there might have been another Maynard who frequented this rec room and he wanted to make sure no one got confused? And "Barb." I envisioned her as a bit butchy, with a puffy vest and a textbook example of *la femme mullet*.

Dell and I slept in separate, adjacent bedrooms on the fifth floor. She was so chaste, so modest, you know? Ppppffft. I argued that it'd be safer for us to stay in the same room, even offered to sleep on the floor all chivalrous-like, but I think she saw right through that pathetic attempt at courtship. I suppose there was a chance the Sloogs would have eventually figured out a way to worm their way up a few flights of stairs and pick a lock or two, but I wasn't too concerned. Did they even have opposable thumbs? Still, I didn't want to wake up one day feeling like I was encased in a Jell-O mold, seconds away from my final breaths. Saw that happen to a guy when the Sloogs first started popping up around town. Not a pretty sight. Even worse were the sounds, like pulling galoshes out of thick, wet mud. I hoped it wouldn't take something as extreme as the threat of imminent immolation for Dell to hop into the sack with me.

"I think we should try to get out of the city," Dell said. She shot the solid burgundy 7-ball into a corner pocket with zero effort. "Maybe we can go somewhere that's in the mountains or the countryside? We're only a couple of hours from Julian or Big Bear. I'm willing to bet there's less danger and—"

"I don't know, Dell. Too risky."

"But don't you think there could be more people hiding out in those regions?"

"Maybe, but who knows if we'll be able to find enough gas to get out there, or even a car we can find the keys for? I sure as hell don't know how to hotwire...do you?"

Dell shook her head. I kept yapping.

"And we could end up stranded. At least we have relatively secure shelter here for now. I doubt there are any people out in the mountains anyway. Even if, we have no way of knowing if they'd be friendly."

"You're certainly not a pessimist, are you?"

"Born and raised. How do we even know what the hell it's going to be like out there once winter hits? It could be even more wonky than it is here. It's your life, your call, but I can tell you right now I'm not taking that chance."

I could see clearly in Dell's face that she was not only displeased with my position, but that she knew I was right. Did she ever admit it, though?

I aimed for the yellow-striped 9-ball, lined up perfectly with a side pocket. I slipped when I hit the cue ball and missed my mark; instead I cracked it right into the 8-ball and set it up perfectly for Dell's shot. Damn.

"Hey, at least we've got each other, though," I said. Dell didn't answer. She could have left and tried her chances on her own, but deep down I suspected she needed me like I did her. Well, maybe not *me* specifically, but some sort of relatively normal human company. It's amazing what companionship can do for your sanity. The Sloogs weren't the sorts of guests you would have invited over for tea and cookies, so she didn't have much choice.

I lit up a crooked cigarette, warm from being squeezed inside my pocket. Dell clucked her tongue at me, then called her pocket for the 8 and sunk that sucker right in.

"You know...those things will kill you," she said.

On the roof. Again. The sun was roasting us raw, but we needed the fresh air. Sunblock streaked our faces like war paint. We were both sitting at the edge of the roof this time, our feet almost kicking together in unison. Could have had the urge to join hands, count to ten, and jump as a pair. The scenery was becoming just a little too familiar. Buildings once bustling with business were empty monoliths. The same stranded vehicles on our side of the block that had been there for weeks, months. They would always be there. I memorized them. Forest green Toyota pick-up. Silver Honda Civic. Convertible Mustang. I took a closer look at the corpses entombed within them, and those were also branded into my memory. The features of their mummified faces slowly weathered away by the elements. The smell like an old can of anchovies left open and hidden on top of a masonry oven.

Our surroundings were too restricting. With comfort came complacency. Mistakes. No Sloogs in sight, so at least that was a bonus. I heard some of them screeching a few blocks away, though. Like witches cackling at their cauldron.

"So, Dell—can I ask you something?"

"I believe you already have."

"You're a psychiatrist, right? Or were." A low rumble came from Dell's throat, like a distant stampede of buffalo on the other side of the prairie.

"Psychologist."

"Same difference."

"No, Adam, it is most certainly *not* the same thing. I have a PsyD, not an M.D. I'm rather offended by the—"

"Okayokayokay. Loud and clear. So did you ever examine anyone's dreams? Like that Sigler Freud guy?"

"Sigmund." Her voice was even gruffer now. She was an old man with an artificial voice box resulting from chronic emphysema.

"That's what I said. So I had this dream once. Literally, once. Only dream I've ever been able to remember my whole life."

"Adam, can't I just have some time to think out here? I really would prefer not to—"

"Dell...seriously. What else are you going to do? It's not like you can bide your time until the next exciting episode of *One Tree Hill*." She seemed to begrudgingly accept this angle, turned back around, and shrugged, so I continued. "I mean, supposedly you're always dreaming during REM, right? I'm not sure why I've been screwed out of my dreams my whole life, but that's beside the point. In this dream—get this—an invisible monster attacks an invisible city full of invisible people. Bizarre, huh? Have you ever heard of anything like that before?"

"I'm not sure I'm getting the gist of this." Dell seemed a little more intrigued. I must have tapped into her primal shrink instincts. "Can you elaborate?"

"Total blankness, you know? The absence of any imagery. Just nothing. And what does 'nothing' look like, exactly? Try to picture that. You can't! You'll still envision something, even if it's just whatever your mind's version of nothingness is. It's impossible to imagine nothing because your brain will still form an image, even if it's not something physical. Right? Even beyond that, who or what created this nothing? There had to be something behind it, right?"

"You've clearly thought about this a great deal."

"It just makes me mental. My dream's so bunk I wasn't even graced with a visual. Just the soundtrack. Lots of screaming, crashing, chaos. Weird, right? What, do you make of that, Doc?"

"Please don't call me 'Doc'."

We were quiet for a bit. Still hovering by the edge of the roof, but we scooted over to the side where the alley was, since there was less direct sunlight. Dell was still, but I couldn't stop kicking my feet against the architecture, staring down at the alleyways of downtown L.A. Rows and rows of filth-ridden, tattered tents lined the walls. I remembered when I had first moved to town and I was doing one of those "off the books" deliveries on my bike. Heading down Main Street, I got lost looking for whatever side street I needed to find. I turned down a dead end and saw a lot of tents just like these. Also saw clusters of strung-out psychos just shambling around. *Night of the Living Crackheads.* Maybe they were trying to figure out which ghetto teepee they were supposed to mosey on back to. Scary shit for sure, but I would have taken that in a heartbeat. At least it had some semblance of normalcy to it.

Dell finally broke the silence. "Given what little I know about you and your dream, I'd say it's just a reflection of how you view yourself. You think no one sees you. Or at least the right people don't." The grin plastered to her face looked sarcastic.

"So this is what my $100 an hour earns? I demand a refund!"

I actually got a laugh out of Dell for that one. Right then, she was almost kind of beautiful. A smile can do that even for the most hardened woman. Her teeth cracked through. Imperfect enough to know she never had braces, but in good enough shape to tell that she hadn't ever needed them. Her complexion had darkened so much that she was in danger of a racial identity crisis. Her ginger curls were sculpted into a permanent bedhead; they had started to form into unintentional matted dreadlocks. She made it work.

"So Dell, have you thought at all about what's going to happen to the human race? Like, who's going to repopulate it? Or if that's even an option at this point?"

"That's a heavy burden."

"Oh, I know. But it might be our unfortunate burden to bear." I winked as I said this. Smooth as a crocodile's tongue.

"I'd rather not have that sort of responsibility on my conscience. It's not like the pickings are plentiful." Dell paused for a few seconds. "No offense. I didn't mean it like—"

"None taken."

Dell smiled; I think she was finally warming up to me.

"I also worry about my body's conditions at my age," she said. "The batteries on my biological clock are moribund. I might be unable to carry a healthy child. The last thing I'd need is to have to try and take care of a Down's Syndrome baby in this world. It's a huge risk."

I finally found my *cojones* and put my arm around her shoulders. I didn't even try to fake a yawn. I gave her shoulder a tiny squeeze.

"Well, what's life without a little risk, right?"

Dell hesitated, barely, then placed her hand on my thigh and squeezed it just firmly enough to convey her intentions.

Or so I thought. Just as quickly, she took her hand away and folded it deeply into the curve of her lap. I started to feel like I was on a failed first date, and there wasn't even any popcorn to focus on.

"That's one of the most potently hypocritical things I've heard exit your mouth," she said. Her voice was a sultry whisper.

"I'm kind of into you, Dell. I can't be all that bad, can I?"

Dell stared off into nothingness, like something had just sucked all of the energy right out of her. She sighed. "I've certainly made worse choices in my life."

"Let's give it a try. We might not have a chance tomorrow or the next day."

"That statement's either extremely sensible or I'm falling victim to early senility. I suppose you have a time in mind?"

"Now's good for me. My calendar's clear."

She stared at me. Not in a romantic way, but more like a "confused as to how I ended up here" sort of way. I figured I should take what I could get.

Dell grazed the palm of her hand against my face, exploring my patchy whiskers. She hovered there for a moment, then stretched up to kiss me. It was kind of a struggle. She was part of the 5'2" crew, just shy of being a dwarf. Was that the politically correct term? Eventually I got the hint and leaned down to reciprocate. Our dry, chafed lips sandpapered each other. Our combined breath practically formed a smoky skull and crossbones above our heads. Not exactly magic, but Little Adam managed to stand at attention. Always reliable.

"You know...I'm ovulating right now," she said, and gave me a coy, playful look. She should have been an actress instead of a psychiatrist.

We stumbled back to her room, which I hoped would be thought of as "our" room for future endeavors. We started peeling our sticky cotton layers off, and the ripe scent of our unshowered bodies wafted through the room like rotten, forgotten fruit discarded behind the bed weeks ago. It did not deter our forced lust. This was probably suitable enough for Piltdown Man, right? I let her get on top since she was so tiny. I noticed her legs hadn't been shaved in God knows how long; the hair tickled me like a clutter of spiders. After a brief game of "Find the Hole," I finally fit myself inside her.

And, of course, I was a total minuteman. Fuck. I knew I should have been using that lotion I had taken from GoodFoods and cashed in on some of my spank bank.

"Shit. Sorry, Dell."

"It's okay. Just take a break. We'll try again in a few. The more the merrier."

"Now that's what I'm talking about."

Weeks later and Dell was not pleased with the results. I think it was weeks. None of the world's calendar-makers had shipped their products out in time for the New Year. Which would have been when, exactly?

"You know what's been starting to freak me out, Dell?"

"No, but I suspect you're going to tell me regardless."

"Let's say—hypothetically—that we do end up having kids. And that we end up with at least one male and one female. What if we really are the last hope for repopulation? Do you realize what that implies?"

Dell just stared at me like I was an amusing little dancing monkey. Fez cap, vest, and all.

"I mean that somewhere down the line, if we never find any other survivors, it's going to have to result in something a little worse than kissin' cousins, you know?"

"You're not making a good case for continuing this relationship."

"I'm just going to head down to GoodFoods and find you another preggo test, okay?"

"Please do. I'm beginning to have some concerns that something's wrong."

"Don't worry. We stick to our schedule, and something's bound to come of it."

"Positive thinking. I appreciate that."

Well, I had to respect her determination. Does it make me a terrible person that I withheld the information that I had a vasectomy when I was twenty-one?

Nah. What's life without a little hope?

ભ⚜ಈ

Chad Stroup *received his MFA in Fiction from San Diego State University. His work has recently been featured in* Fiction International *and the* Grey Matter Press *anthology* Splatterlands, *and a poem of his was selected for the inaugural* Horror Writers Association Poetry Showcase. *He has been nominated for the* AWP Intro Journals Award *as well as* the Pushcart Prize. *His blog, Subvertbia, is a showcase of some of his short fiction and poetry.*
http://subvertbia.blogspot.com/. https://www.facebook.com/ChadStroupWriter.

Necromancy

Richard H. Fay

mouldering crypts
tombs desecrated
necromancer's realm

sanguineous ink
incantations scripted
necromancer's tome

macabre magic
apparitions questioned
necromancer's art

stolen coffin
corpse reanimated
necromancer's slave

muculent mass
tentacles writhe
necromancer's pet

mephitic fumes
miasma suffocates
necromancer's death

Richard H. Fay *currently resides in upstate New York with his wife and two cats. Formerly a laboratory technician-turned-home educator, Richard now spends his days juggling numerous writing and art projects. History, myth, folklore, and legend serve as inspiration for his creative endeavours. Many of the fruits of his labour have appeared in various e-zines, print magazines, and anthologies.*

For Once I Woke

A. W. Gifford

For once I woke and felt his presence,
I saw his twisted form beside my bed.
Shadows, I thought and nothing more.
I closed my eyes and went back to sleep.

For once I woke and heard his voice:
"Come with me and you'll feel no pain."
Imagination, I thought and nothing more.
I closed my eyes and went back to sleep.

For once I woke and saw his face,
I looked into his eyes and saw the truth.
Now, I cannot sleep for I know too much.
Now, I must be sure to never wake again.

A.W. Gifford *is an internationally unknown author who gets many of his story ideas from the nightmares of his wife, Jennifer. She too is an author of dark fiction, but she refuses to write her own nightmares as she fears doing so will make them come true. Story ideas also come to him from his dogs, the dust bunnies under the bed and one very helpful garden gnome.*

He is an editor at Bête Noire Magazine and Dark Opus Press and his work has appeared in numerous magazines, anthologies and was once spotted stalking the woods of the Pacific Northwest.

He, on the other hand, can be found stalking the woods in the northern suburbs of Detroit, while his wife and daughter huddle in the warmth of the house with their two dogs and the aforementioned dust bunnies.

Chronological Disorder

H. L. Fullerton

These are the facts: time cannot fly, only rupture; it takes four minutes and eleven seconds to cook the perfect soft-boiled egg; and — whether he knows it or not — Hap Germaine murdered Dorit Pruce. The rest is nothing but a stack of waiting photographs. Flip, flip, shuffle, flip.

Snapshot. A balding man in a ratty blue bathrobe — Hap Germaine — stares, brow furrowed, eyes pinched, into the top drawer of his tallboy dresser — walnut, Mission-styled. One hand grips the square pull; the other disappears into the drawer, its elbow cocked as if it's been caught rummaging. Balls of socks peek over the drawer's edge; one white lump lies near Hap's slippered feet.

Snapshot. Hap — still puzzled, still standing at his dresser — holds up a tiny hourglass capped with blue ends. The presence of the timer in his sock drawer confounds him. He lives alone; his wife Patty's been dead two decades; he has no housekeeper. He thinks it could've come from one of Patty's old board games that's moldering in the pantry — but didn't hers all have yellow ends? He wonders if this is the start of Alzheimer's and if he should double-check that he placed the milk in the fridge and not the cupboard when he finished his cereal.

Snapshot. Yard sale. Tables and boxes form shaky rows. The grass needs to be mowed. Mid-frame, a woman — mid-forties, sunglasses and straw hat — wearing a floral skirt digs through a cluttered cardboard box. A plastic pig sits next to the box, posing for the camera. Grin, piggy, grin.

Snapshot. Hap bent over a gas stove, blue flame licking the bottom of a red enameled pot. On the freckled formica countertop, barely clearing the folds of Hap's checkered shirt, peeks a disc blue cap and a glint of light reflecting off something glass. Hap's decided to use his discovery to boil eggs. His preferred consistency takes two turns and a tap of the timer to finish. He never lets all the grains fall to one side. Hap doesn't believe in wasting time and he is all too aware that, for him, time is running out. Grains of sand trickle through the hourglass, match the lub-dub of his heart. Tick, tick...

Close-up. Egg timer lying on its side atop a smooth dark walnut finish. Three-quarters of the sand lies like a tiny dune in one half; the rest pools like a drought-stricken lake in the other. There is a shadow or a symbol on the blue cap. A flame, a crack, maybe a faded number — it's hard to tell.

Snapshot. An angered man in a red three piece suit stands in a wood-paneled courtroom covered in melting clocks. At his feet, lie a collection of black filigreed arrows — some bent, some broken. A woman in a white dress is exiting the room. If this were a painting — it's not — it'd be called, *Time Waits for No One*, or maybe *A Devil of an Ex*.

Flip, flip. Hap in the kitchen wearing a different shirt. Hap eating from a Dresden egg cup at a scarred maple table. Hap cooking, Hap eating, showering, puttering, Hap, Hap, Hap. And always a hint of blue, a curve of glass, a drop of sand.

Snapshot. Hap drains eggs over the sink, a puff a steam eclipsing his features, making him look years younger. A bulging face — no, a grease stain on the wallpaper behind him.

Flip. A cinderblock room — whitewashed — perhaps a church basement. A child's desk, a kitchen chair with a plastic yellow cushions. A jumble of clocks, a few watches, decorate the desktop. A middle-aged woman's hand grasps the edge of a pop-novelty clock missing the minute hand.

Snapshot. Hap hunched in the pantry — sage green with once-white trim — over a shelf — middling high — of board games. Clutched in his fist is an egg timer, held horizontally. A yellow box top with green lettering, corners taped, is raised. Above him is the good china, tiny rosebud dots; then cardboard boxes with black marker scrawl. One says: Keepsakes. Below him are an array of cleaning supplies and a rusted watering can. He has checked and rechecked every game. None is missing a timer. He's almost convinced he doesn't have dementia. But then how did the timer make its way into his sock drawer? And why does his heart beat faster every time he uses it? Maybe it's time to visit the cardiologist. Doc'll probably tell him to steer clear of eggs, track his sugar, eat more fiber. But Hap thinks maybe cholesterol ain't a bad way to go. Also, it might be time to donate Patty's things. Where have the years gone?

Snapshot. A wall filled with assorted hourglasses, varying heights, some etched with odd marks, a few gaps where others have gone missing. The heel of a shoe and a stripe of pant leg—red—seems almost super-imposed on the bottom right edge.

Snapshot. A sign with a big blocky arrow: Estate Sale Today.

Close-up of a metal tabletop—brown with cream flourishes. Water marked, edge peeling back. A man's wrinkled hand. A yellowed band. An hourglass on its side. A bubble mars a patch of glass—as if the glassblower made a mistake. You can almost hear the television in the background.

Snapshot. Hap on his front porch, swing off to one side, brown box marked *Keepsakes* in his arms. His back is straight and there's swag in his step.

Snapshot. A nearly deserted outdoor café, chairs askew as if pushed back suddenly and vacated. A woman walking by, wearing a toile dress with figures moving on the fabric—drinking tea, climbing mountains, slumped over office desks—tiny clocks counting down. Freshly scripted across her arm is Tempus Regit. Her ring finger sports a white band of flesh, unkissed by sun. On the sidewalk about to be crushed by her shoe is a trail of broken arrows.

Snapshot. A folding table laden with boxes, vintage women's clothes, and children's games. A yellow box with green lettering stands out amongst more faded rectangles of whites and blues. Atop the pile is an egg timer with blue-capped ends, sands running free...

Hap Germain is sitting on his porch swing when Dorit Pruce's car pulls to the curb in front of his bungalow. Her eyes are hidden behind sunglasses, her hair tucked under a wide-brimmed hat. As she beelines for the board games, her canvas bag disappears into her skirt's folds. The flowers on her skirt remind Hap of the roses on Patty's china. His eyes tear up a bit and he looks away. So unfair that his wife is dead and reminders of her can walk around, oblivious and breathing.

Dorit's eyes catch on the timer, the distortion in its glass. She picks it up for a closer look. The white sand is piled in a tiny pyramid.

Snap. As she lifts the hourglass, an invisible grain of sand shakes free from its neck and falls like a snowflake. Dorit's fall is much noisier. She crashes to the ground, boxes avalanching down upon her.

Hap spies the rose-wearing woman dead on his lawn and thinks, *Time's up.*

H.L. Fullerton *writes fiction — mostly speculative, occasionally about dev-ils and details — which is sometimes published in places like* Buzzy, Penum-bra, *DarkFuse's* Horror D'oeuvres, *and* Bête Noire.

www.ingramcontent.com/pod-product-compliance
Lightning Source LLC
Chambersburg PA
CBHW071217130626
46555CB00004B/1746